The Only Living Cavewoman You Will Ever Meet

Written by
Dr. Cleo Molina

Illustrations by
Carolyn Flores

DEDICATION

This book is dedicated to my mother, Isabel, who asked me to tell her story when she was in the last years of a very long life and to my grandmother Clotilde who gave birth in a cave.

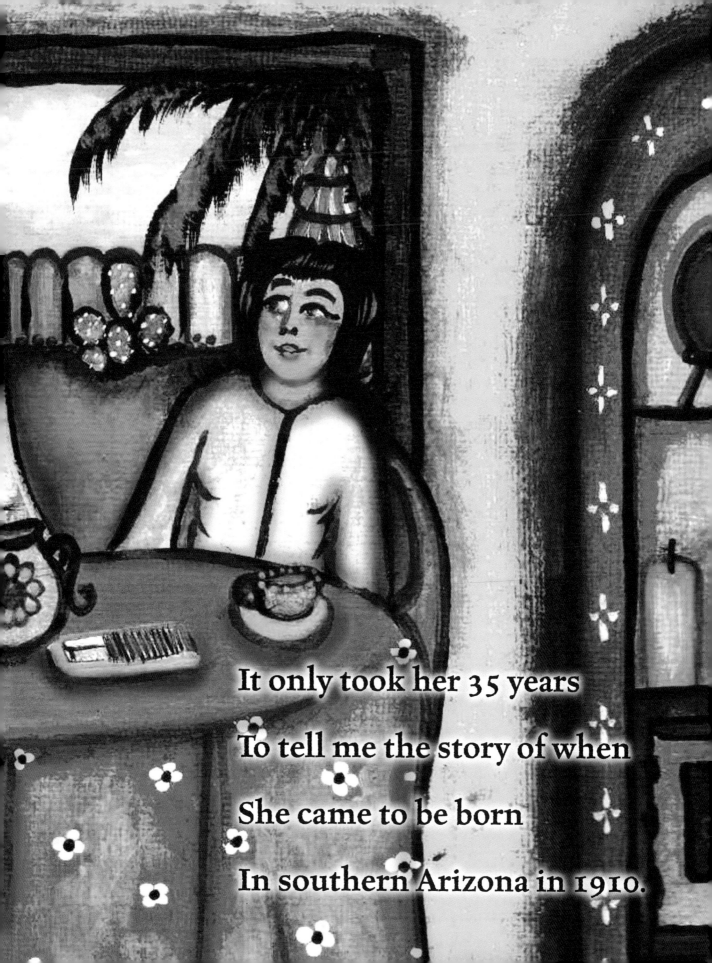

It only took her 35 years
To tell me the story of when
She came to be born
In southern Arizona in 1910.

"How old are you, Mom?"

I asked many times,

My little girl self

Thought the answer was mine.

But she didn't like revealing her age

"You're as old as you feel," she'd say,

"So I'm as old as Jack Benny – '39'.

"Now go find your *primas* and play."

So I did what you do

When you're a curious kid

And looked in the boxes

And files that she hid.

I found her baptismal certificate,

And the names of her family,

But when and where she was born

No estaba allí.

Then one starlit evening

When sipping her favorite champagne,

She told the story of how

Her familia from Zacatecas they came.

Just one covered wagon

Carried all that they had;

Two families leaving their homeland

During a war that left them

Uprooted and sad.

Julio y Clotilde and their three young sons;

Clotilde expecting - a daughter she hoped.

Juan y Maria with their little ones

All snuggled together to keep out the cold...

One dime per adult

Was all that they paid

To cross the border from *Méjico*

Into the United States.

They came in December

During the harshest of times;

The two brothers, Julio y Juan,

Hoped to work in the mines.

They'd heard that Mexican people

Were welcome to come

And jobs were plentiful

And so were some homes.

But no houses were found

In their new country in winter

And Julio's young wife

Was soon due to deliver.

So finding a cave

That could provide them some shelter

The brothers started to build

Adobe *casitas* from mud and water.

But babies don't wait

Till times are the best.

Labor began for Clotilde

Putting Maria, her midwife, to the test.

With no other help

To deliver her *bebé*

She put her trust in her God,

Her sister-in-law, *y La Virgen de Guadalupe*.

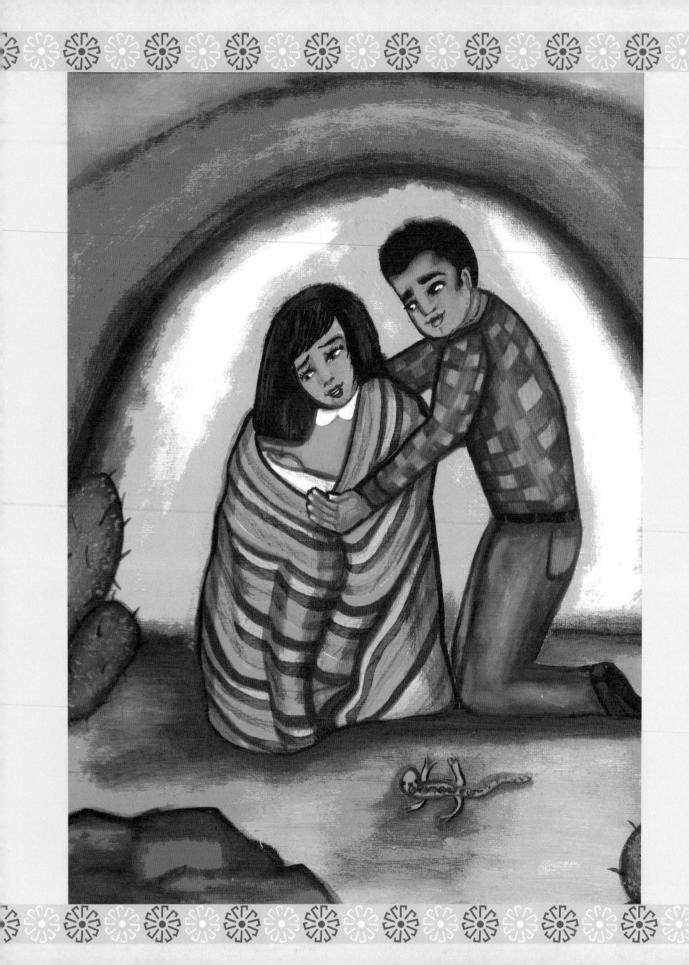

On January 6 in the year 1910,

El Día de Los Tres Reyes Magos,

Niña Isabel was born in a cave –

Just like *El Niño Jesus*!

"I didn't tell you my story

When you were a girl,

I was afraid you would think

You had the strangest *mamá*

In the whole wide world."

So now that her secret was out
She said of her remarkable birth,
"I'm the only living cavewoman
You'll meet on this earth!"

ABOUT THE AUTHOR

Cleo Molina, Ed.D., is an educator and consultant whose bilingual, bicultural upbringing (Mexican and Anglo heritage) ingrained in her a passion for understanding, describing and bridging cultural differences. She has written primarily for the academic and faith-based sectors and is now focusing on capturing her multicultural history and spirituality in poetry and fiction. She lives in Tukwila, WA with her husband and the ancient poodle that she inherited from her mother Isabel. Cleo promised her mother, prior to her death at age ninety-nine, that she would tell her story and take care of Bonnie, the poodle. *The Only Living Cavewoman You Will Ever Meet* is Cleo's first effort at keeping the first part of the promise. Bonnie makes sure she keeps the second part.

ABOUT THE ARTIST

Carolyn Flores is an award winning artist who lives in New Mexico with her husband and three children. Her love for art was discovered at a young age and her inspiration comes from her rich New Mexican heritage. She participates in juried art shows all over the Southwest and has won many awards and accolades for her paintings. She is well-known for her vibrant use of color and her beautiful portrayal of ethnic/Latino themes. Her art is very diverse exploring themes such as spirituality, religious icons, popular culture, day of the dead, famous figures, and cultural practices. Her unique style was self-taught. She enjoys sharing her art with adults and children alike.

HISTORICAL AND SOCIAL REFERENCES

This section provides general information about historical and social references as well as basic translations for some of the Spanish words included in the story.

- Arizona was a territory in 1910. It became a state in 1912.

- Jack Benny was a very well-known and beloved comedian during the mid-twentieth century. One of his standing jokes (and he had many!) was insisting he was thirty-nine years old on every birthday. (See Biography for Jack Benny at http://www.imbd.com/name/nm0000912/bio)

- *Primas* – girl cousins

- *No estaba allí* – was not there

- *Familia* – family

- Zacatecas – a state in the north central part of Mexico

- Civil War – look up the Mexican Revolution, 1910-1920 in your local library or online.

- *Casitas* – little houses

- *La Virgen de Guadalupe* – beloved patroness of Mexico. People throughout the Americas and the world are especially devoted to her because of her advocacy for poor and disenfranchised people and care for the infirm. She first appeared on a hill in Tepeyác, near Mexico City, on December 9, 1531.

- *El Día de los Tres Reyes Magos* – Three Kings Day or Epiphany, a major holiday celebrated in Mexico and throughout Latin America on January 6.

Made in the USA
Charleston, SC
15 December 2012